A Note to Parents and Caregivers:

Read-it! Readers are for children who are just starting on the amazing road to reading. These beautiful books support both the acquisition of reading skills and the love of books.

 The PURPLE LEVEL presents basic topics and objects using high frequency words and simple language patterns.

 The RED LEVEL presents familiar topics using common words and repeating sentence patterns.

 The BLUE LEVEL presents new ideas using a larger vocabulary and varied sentence structure.

 The YELLOW LEVEL presents more challenging ideas, a broad vocabulary, and wide variety in sentence structure.

 The GREEN LEVEL presents more complex ideas, an extended vocabulary range, and expanded language structures.

 The ORANGE LEVEL presents a wide range of ideas and concepts using challenging vocabulary and complex language structures.

When sharing a book with your child, read in short stretches, pausing often to talk about the pictures. Have your child turn the pages and point to the pictures and familiar words. And be sure to reread favorite stories or parts of stories.

There is no right or wrong way to share books with children. Find time to read with your child, and pass on the legacy of literacy.

Adria F. Klein, Ph.D.
Professor Emeritus
California State University
San Bernardino, California

Editor: Christianne Jones
Designer: Amy Bailey Muehlenhardt
Page Production: Tracy Kaehler
Creative Director: Keith Griffin
Editorial Director: Carol Jones
The illustrations in this book were created digitally.

Picture Window Books
5115 Excelsior Boulevard
Suite 232
Minneapolis, MN 55416
877-845-8392
www.picturewindowbooks.com

Printed in the United States of America.

Library of Congress Cataloging-in-Publication Data
Kalz, Jill.
Bears on ice / by Jill Kalz ; illustrated by Troy Olin.
p. cm. — (Read-it! readers)
Summary: When three bears go fishing in a little house on the ice and catch only one
fish, they have a good time eating what they have brought in their backpacks.
ISBN 1-4048-1577-5 (hardcover)
[1. Fishing—Fiction. 2. Bears—Fiction.] I. Olin, Troy, ill. II. Title. III. Series.

PZ7.K12655Bdu 2005
[E]—dc22   2005021441

Bears on Ice

by Jill Kalz
illustrated by Troy Olin

Special thanks to our advisers for their expertise:

Adria F. Klein, Ph.D.
Professor Emeritus, California State University
San Bernardino, California

Susan Kesselring, M.A.
Literacy Educator
Rosemount–Apple Valley–Eagan (Minnesota) School District

PICTURE WINDOW BOOKS
Minneapolis, Minnesota

A little house sat on a lake.

Don, Roman, and Ray were fishing inside.

They drilled a hole in the ice.

They baited their hooks.

They waited for the fish to bite.

But no fish came.

The bears played cards for peanuts and watched the hole. Don won all of the peanuts.

But no fish came.

They drank hot chocolate and
watched the hole.
Roman ate all of
the marshmallows.

But no fish came.

They told stories about superheroes and watched the hole. Ray pretended to fly.

But no fish came.

Suddenly, Don's fishing pole jumped.
The bears jumped, too.

They danced and cheered.
They had finally caught a fish!

But one fish wasn't enough for three hungry bears. Don didn't know what to do.

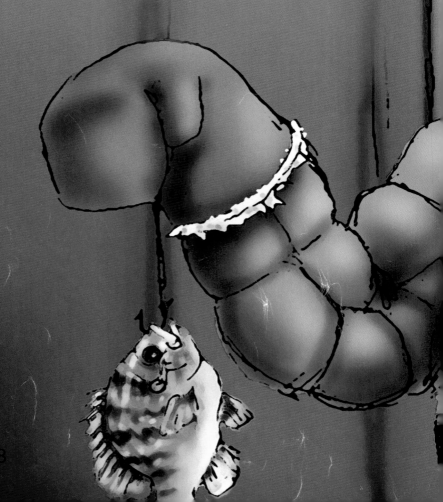

19

Roman opened his backpack. He had crackers shaped like fish.

Ray opened his backpack. He had yellow and blue candy shaped like fish.

The three bears shared all kinds
of fish. The little house on the lake
was filled with happy friends.

More *Read-it!* Readers

Bright pictures and fun stories help you practice your reading skills. Look for more books at your level.

At the Beach 1-4048-0651-2
The Bossy Rooster 1-4048-0051-4
Dust Bunnies 1-4048-1168-0
Flying with Oliver 1-4048-1583-X
Frog Pajama Party 1-4048-1170-2
Jack's Party 1-4048-0060-3
The Lifeguard 1-4048-1584-8
The Playground Snake 1-4048-0556-7
Recycled! 1-4048-0068-9
Robin's New Glasses 1-4048-1587-2
The Sassy Monkey 1-4048-0058-1
Tuckerbean 1-4048-1591-0
What's Bugging Pamela? 1-4048-1189-3

Looking for a specific title or level? A complete list of *Read-it!* Readers is available on our Web site:
www.picturewindowbooks.com